The Rescue

Written by Alan Durant
Illustrated by Steve James

Collins

"Hang on, Tom!" a voice shouted from above me. But I didn't know how long I could hang on. "Help is on the way!" It was Alex, my best friend, who was shouting.

We'd been having such a great time. How could it all have gone so wrong?

It was a sunny day. Alex and I had decided to take my dog Stan for a walk along the cliff top. The view was amazing from up there. I was looking over the edge of the cliff when my foot slipped from under me.

"Agh!" I cried in panic, as the ground suddenly fell away.

Terrified, I slid down the rock face. Somehow, I managed to grab hold of a narrow ledge.

I was clinging on to the rock, but I was starting to get cramp in my hands. I could feel my fingers slipping – I was losing my grip.

"Hold on, Tom!" Alex called again. "Help won't be long."

But how long could I hold on? Soon I would drop on to the rocks below.

Some gulls flew by me. If only I had wings, I thought. My legs dangled in the air, and I felt faint and dizzy. I was so tired. "Give up, let go," said a soft voice inside my head.

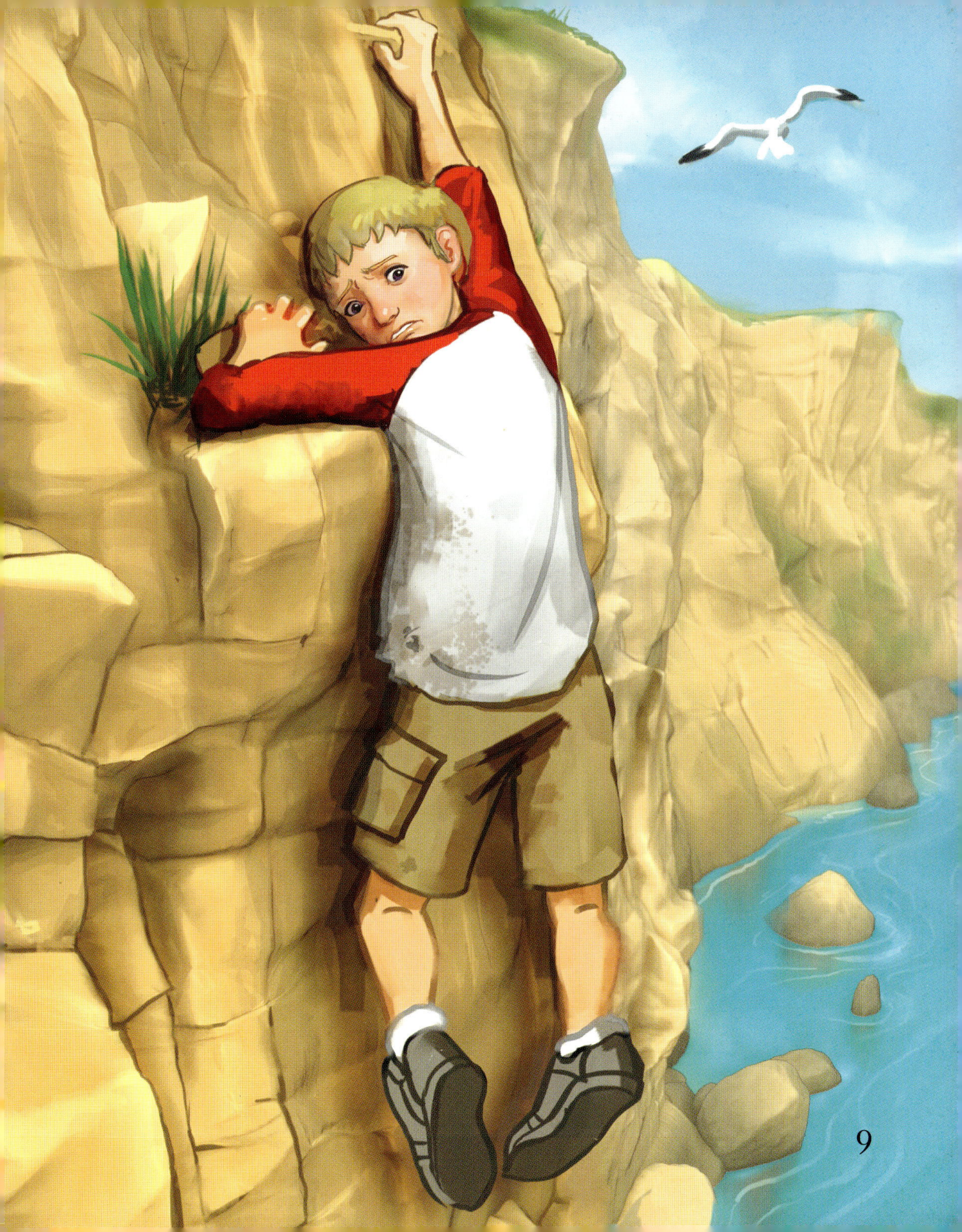

But there was another voice. It said, "Keep holding on. You must fight to save yourself."

I was in pain from head to toe. I wouldn't look down and I couldn't look up. Then I heard a dog bark. "Woof, woof!" It was Stan. He was telling me to hang on!

I stared at the sheer rock in front of me. I willed myself to be strong. But it was no use. It was so hot and I was getting weak. I was going to fall. I was going to die.

13

And then I heard it. First, there was a hum in the air, then a throb and a whirr. I couldn't see anything but the noise was getting louder, closer.

I could picture blades spinning round and round.
It was so loud that my ears hurt.

A man in a harness banged against the rock beside me. He inched towards me, swinging on a rope.

"Almost there, lad," he said. He put a belt round my waist. Then he pulled it tight. "Now, let go!" he shouted.

I still held on. What if my mind was playing tricks on me? What if I fell?

"Let go!" the man called once more – and this time I did.

For a moment, I was treading air. I couldn't breathe. I flapped my arms. My head rolled. Then I smiled as I saw I was going up, not down. I was rising towards the helicopter. I could see Alex and Stan on the cliff, and I waved and grinned. I was safe.

I'd been rescued.

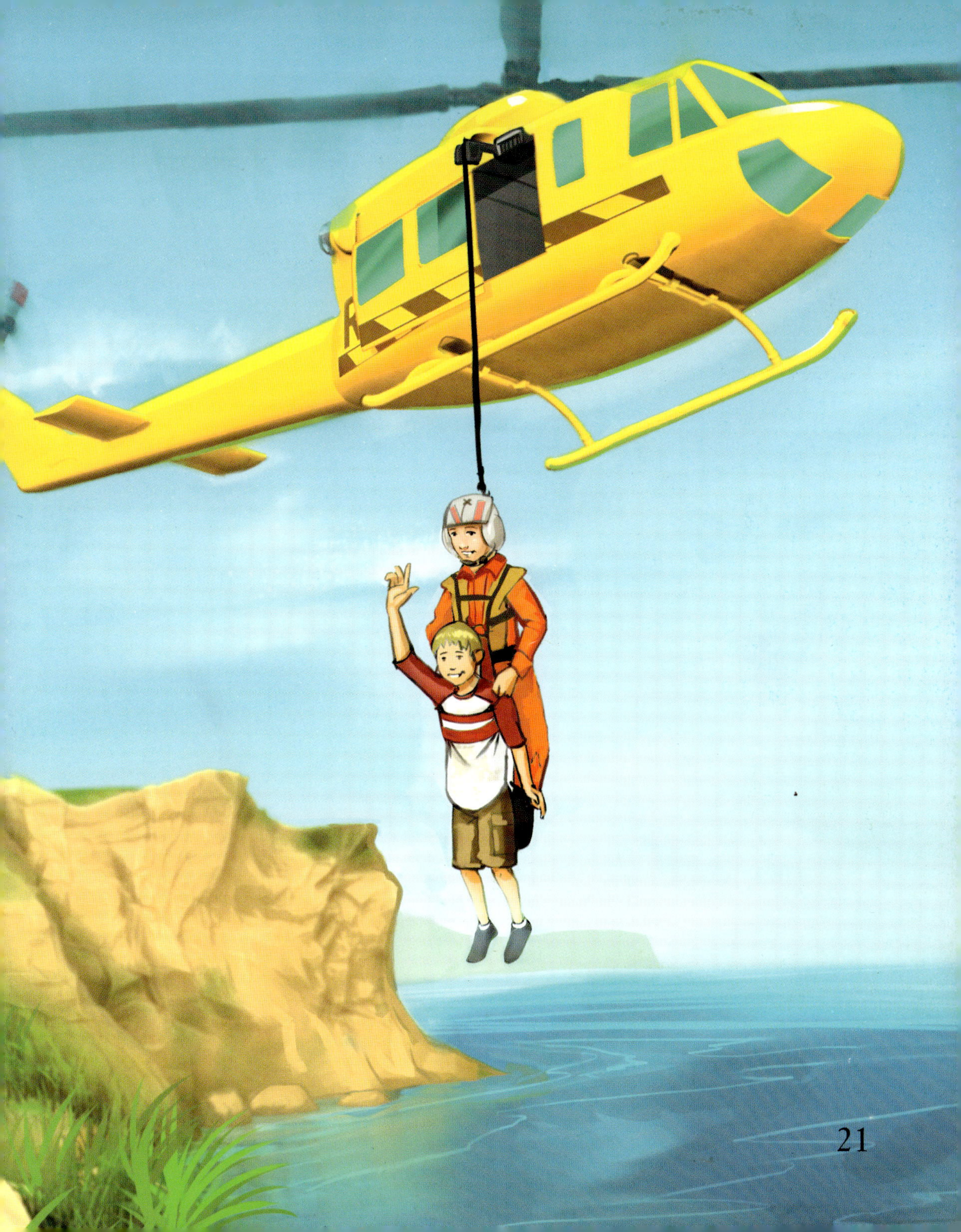

Tom's feelings

I willed myself to be strong.

"Give up, and let go," said a soft voice inside my head.

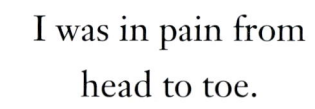

I was in pain from head to toe.

Terrified, I slid down the rock face.

What if my mind was playing tricks on me?

What if I fell?

I waved and grinned. I was safe.

Ideas for reading

Written by Gillian Howell
Primary Literacy Consultant

Learning objectives: (*reading objectives correspond with Turquoise band; all other objectives correspond with Diamond band*) read independently and with increasing fluency longer and less familiar texts; understand underlying themes, causes and points of view; understand how writers use different structures to create coherence and impact; improvise using a range of drama strategies and conventions to explore themes such as hopes, fears and desires

Curriculum links: Citizenship

Interest words: rescue, ledge, faint, voice, fight, sheer, whirr, harness, helicopter

Resources: internet, ICT, whiteboard

Word count: 484

Getting started

- Read the title together and discuss the cover illustration. Ask the children what they think is happening and what sort of rescue they think the story will be about. Make a note of their ideas on the whiteboard.
- Turn to the back cover and read the blurb together. Point out the first person narrator and ask them how the last sentence makes them feel.

Reading and responding

- Turn to pp2-3 and ask the children to read aloud. Ask the children to say what they know about the story so far and to speculate on what might have gone wrong.
- Stop at p9 and ask the children to say how they would feel if they were in the same position as Tom. Encourage them to describe the thoughts that might be going through their heads.
- Ask the children to read to the end of the story quietly. Praise children for using an expressive tone in response to the tension in the text.